WARNING

This book contains sexually explicit scenes and adult language. It may be considered offensive to some readers. This book is for sale to adults ONLY.

* * * * * * * * * * * * * * * * *

Please store your files wisely where they cannot be accessed by underage readers.

ISBN-13: 978-1987863826
ISBN-10: 1987863828

Other Books by Darla Dunbar:

<u>The Romeo Alpha BBW Paranormal Shifter Romance Series</u>

Amanda Walker thinks that she has a normal and boring life. That is until after her 24th birthday. Everything changes when she meets the man who says he was supposed to be her husband. Denying everything the man says, she fights him every step of the way. But after he kidnaps her, Amanda discovers that there are some things about her family that her parents kept a secret all these years. Among the history of the family she learns secrets she thought only happened in story books. Can Amanda tell the difference between truth and lies or is she this mysterious woman that holds the key to a legacy?

<u>Romeo Alpha Blood Lines Romance Series</u>

Twenty-four years have passed in relative peace for Amanda and Romeo. They've raised five children into adulthood and are thoroughly enjoying their lives as the Alpha King and Queen of the werewolves. At twenty-four, Sarina is just stepping into her powers and will be ripe for mating when her birthday comes in two weeks. What no one knows is the danger that lurks just outside their tight knit community. Romeo has made peace with the other clans and has enjoyed that peace, but it will all come crashing down around him when his oldest daughter comes of age to take a mate.

The Alpha Feud BBW Paranormal Shifter Romance Series

Eliza's life consisted of reporting on boring, crowd-pleasing events, like their country livestock fair. With the arrival of two handsome brothers, the lives of Eliza and her best friend, Melissa, are shaken to the core. For Eliza, the arrival of this new man becomes a test of her relationship with her current boyfriend, who she's been happily living with for over six years. Does Hayden, a complete stranger, really wield the power to make Eliza reconsider her relationship with Andrew?

The Alpha Packed BBW Paranormal Shifter Romance Series

Darlene has led a quiet life since suffering through a terrible break-up. She wants nothing more than to spend her time in front of the TV, away from any sort of trouble. But all that goes down the drain when handsome, rugged and rough Idris comes into her life. He is a werewolf on the lookout for his missing pack leader. Darlene quickly finds herself pulled towards this mysterious man and at the same time finds herself falling deeper and deeper into the world of the supernatural.

The Mind Talker Paranormal Romance Series

Ananda finds herself on the run and she's not alone. With help from Jared, a stranger that she just met, the two evade capture by an organization that is intent on hunting her kind. Ananda and Jared are able to read minds. When an unfortunate incident happened involving a disturbed individual that resulted in the death of his schoolmates, the secret organization decided to take action.

<u>The Leather Satchel Paranormal Romance Series</u>

Valtina is stuck in Middle World, unable to pass on to The Afterlife. In order to redeem herself from past deeds done, she must help bring romance back into the world and stop The Dark Side from destroying love in its entirety. Following orders issued by Ladaya and armed with a leather satchel filled with the appropriate tools and weapons, Valtina embraces each mission with enthusiasm.

Get the latest update on new releases from the author at:

https://darladunbar.com/newsletter/

This book is Part Two of "The Daemon Paranormal Romance Chronicles"

Book 1 - The Awakening

Phoebe grew up not knowing her mother. The stranger, Apollo Mikos, claimed to know her mother. After that day, Phoebe's life would change forever.

Book 2 - The Shifter

Phoebe is surprised when her dog, Ace, shows up from nowhere. She is on a mission with Apollo to kill the Qilin. That is the only way that the true leader of daemons will emerge.

Book 3 - Forgotten

Juno has been stirring up trouble that has prolonged the infighting among the daemons. In order to get her to stop, Phoebe agrees to give up a year of her memories. But making deals with a siren is never a good thing. Without her memories, Phoebe's romantic relationship with Supay no longer exists. Instead, she leaves Supay for Apollo.

Book 4 - The Siren's Trap

The unsuspecting couple, Phoebe and Supay, made a deal with Juno to stop the infighting among the daemons. But at what price? An entire year was wiped clean from Phoebe's mind. Now Phoebe was with Apollo. Desperate to get her back, Supay considers Juno's new deal. Is it worth the price to pay for the dubious result? To win back Phoebe's love, Supay will need to be unfaithful to her.

Book 5 - Exposed

Hiding away in Peru, Supay and Phoebe start their own family, away from the chaos and the daemon infighting. Meanwhile, Apollo, heart-broken and lost, is lured into another one of Juno's schemes. Making deals with a siren never turns out right. If Apollo accepts the deal, the love of his life may resent him for the rest of his natural life. If he doesn't take the deal, she is lost to him forever.

Book 6 - The Beginning

As preparations for the war between daemons are underway, everyone must begin to choose. Siding temporarily with Apollo, Juno has a moment to look back on her life and figure out how she arrived at this moment. As she sifts through memories of the past, a specific dark stranger stands out. How far will young Juno go with her new love? More importantly, will her mother, Circe, discover the secret tryst?

Book 7 - The Treachery

Having broken the cardinal rule of the sirens, Juno must take action to save her own life and the life of her unborn child. In order to keep her secret safe from the sisterhood, she must kill her lover and conceal her shame. Will Juno betray the sisterhood and save her lover or will she remain loyal by slaying him instead?

Book 8 - Duplicity

Juno's mother, Circe, discovers her lies and gives her an ultimatum to fix everything. As Juno races against the clock to protect her loved ones from Circe, she makes a final choice that could leave her perpetually unhappy. Left to wander the world alone, Juno realizes that freedom means nothing if there is no one to share it with. The nature of Juno's vendetta—and the means she achieves it with—are finally revealed.

Book 9 - Reconnaissance

As Juno's hunt for the daemon's fortress unfolds, Apollo is left alone wondering if she will truly return to him. Will Juno be able to resist her base instincts? More importantly, will she be able to get to the fortress and return without being spotted? Discover how Juno's stealth mission works out.

Book 10 - The Interrogation

Juno tries to hide her rising fear in the presence of her captors. As her fear mounts, she holds on to the hope that Phoebe or Supay will take pity on her. Before that can happen, she has to come clean to Supay about her past. Could he possibly forgive her for what she has done? Will Juno remain faithful to Apollo or will her siren urges take over? Discover how the confrontation with Supay unfolds.

The Daemon Paranormal Romance Chronicles

The Shifter

Book Two

By Darla Dunbar

Copyright Revelry Publishing 2015

Table of Contents

Chapter One 1
Chapter Two 7
Chapter Three 12
Chapter Four 15
Other Books by Darla Dunbar 28
About the Author - Darla Dunbar 29
Connect with Darla Dunbar 30

Chapter One

WALKING OUT of the hotel room, Phoebe jumped back in surprise. Her dog, Ace, ran up to her. "Ace! What are you doing here?" She leaned down to pet him. "Come inside with me and we will get you something to eat."

Bringing him inside with her, she glanced over at Apollo. She met his questioning eyes with a shrug. "I have no clue how he got here. It seems impossible, but here he is."

Apollo shrugged. "Weirder things have happened. I guess we can just bring him along with us. Having him could help." Standing up, he grabbed the bag of weapons and restraints. Together, they left the room and got in the car.

Parking near the jade shop, the pair sipped coffee as they waited for Qilin to close the shop. They inched the car along behind her as she went to a park. The sunlight was quickly fading away and few people were in the park. Quickly, they got out of the car and followed Qilin into a clearing. Although they walked in absolute silence, Qilin turned around.

"I knew you were there. This is your last chance to turn back. Are you ready?" She widened her stance and stood confidently in front of them. Phoebe stepped back so that Apollo could do what he came for.

Grabbing a dagger out of the bag, Apollo nodded. "I am ready if you are." As soon as he finished the sentence, Qilin became a blazing ball of fire. Flames radiated from her arms and curled into balls within her hands. Throwing the fire at Apollo, she moved forward. Apollo ducked the flames and tried to get into an offensive position.

Ace whined next to Phoebe. Leaning down, she patted his head reassuringly. In reality, she was shaking in fear. Still unused to the world of daemons, the fiery daemon before her was a frightening surprise. She felt less terrible about the possibility of Qilin's death. The daemon before her was far from defenseless. Before this moment, how many other potential leaders had tried to kill Qilin and failed?

Qilin threw another ball of fire and it singed Apollo's heels. The grass in the clearing was quickly becoming torched by their fight. Ball after ball of fire was thrown and Apollo managed to shrug it off without any difficulties. Unfortunately, he was unable to stand for long enough to get close to her. Too late, he realized that he should have just used a gun. Rolling away from another ball of fire, he quickly darted in the opposite direction. The sudden change of direction surprised the Qilin, and she let the ball of fire go too soon. It released from her hand and flew directly toward Phoebe. Apollo either did not notice where the fire was headed or did not care. He adjusted his stance and lifted the dagger behind his head to throw it.

At the same time, the fire came toward Phoebe and she found herself unable to move. Ace pushed his mistress away from the flame, but his leg was singed by the blaze. Across the clearing, Apollo released the dagger and it sailed into Qilin's heart. Instantaneously, the fire that surrounded Qilin went out. Falling to the ground, she moved feebly as the life left her body.

Phoebe's paralysis left her as the danger passed. Leaning down, she petted Ace and tried to look at his singed leg. When she touched the leg, the dog's head fell back and she realized that he had passed out from pain. Phoebe started to glance up to see how Apollo was doing when she felt something warm against her leg. Right next to her, Ace was quickly transforming into the figure of a man. Stepping back in shock, she stumbled and fell on to the ground. The naked figure before her was Supay.

Moments passed and Phoebe could not say anything. Across the field, Apollo managed to walk toward the weapons bag and pick it up. In front of Phoebe, Supay opened his eyes. Looking down at his leg, he realized that he was no longer a dog. Bashfully, he tried to stand up and fell back down. His burned leg would not support his body.

Anger and disbelief contorted Phoebe's face. "You were Ace the whole time?" Ace had been her dog for years. She had bathed him, changed in front of him, and walked him every day.

Wincing, Supay tried to find what to say. "Yes, but it isn't what you think. I was just trying to protect you."

Apollo approached and gestured at Supay. "What is he doing here? Was he Ace?"

Phoebe did not take her eyes off of Supay. "Well, let's hear it. This better be a good explanation or I won't give you clothes and help you get to a hospital."

Supay paused and framed his thoughts. "I just needed to be near you and protect you. A few years ago, I heard that the Qilin was born and knew someone would go after it. I was going to protect her but quickly discovered that she had no need for protection. You saw her. She's like a one-man army. In my search, I discovered you and your unique talents. I knew that someone would come looking for you in order to find the Qilin, and I wanted to make sure that you were safe. You don't possess any talents that would protect you, and many of the people looking for the Qilin are questionable characters. If I thought you would have believed me and allowed me to stay at your side in any other form, I would have."

Reaching his arm around Phoebe's back, Apollo held her possessively close. "That isn't an excuse. I kept her safe."

"No, you didn't." Supay shot back. "I just saw you choose killing the Qilin over saving Phoebe's life. This quest and a role as a leader matter more to you than Phoebe. You know it, so don't bother pretending to be some white knight."

Apollo moved aggressively forward, but Phoebe stopped him. Instead, Apollo pointed accusingly at Supay. "It isn't true. I love her. You're one to talk about moral qualms, considering you spent years watching her in secret."

Phoebe was speechless. All of these years, he had tried to protect her by violating her privacy. She was never getting a pet again. "How can you even justify this?"

Supay pointed at Apollo. "He isn't any better. Did he tell you what his talent is?" Apollo lurched forward and put his hands around Supay's neck. Supay didn't even put up resistance to his attack. Phoebe dashed forward and pulled Apollo off of Supay.

"What does he mean, Apollo?" she asked. Apollo didn't respond, so Supay spoke for him.

"Apollo can control the minds of other people." Apollo started to say something and Supay held up his hand to stop him. "I'm sorry, that isn't quite right. He plants suggestions in their minds. If it's something they were totally against, like robbing a bank, the person won't do it. But if the person is even partially accepting of the idea, it works."

Phoebe paused. When they first met, she had accidentally touched Apollo's hand several times. Each time, she saw an image of them having sex. Phoebe looked at Apollo. "So it's true? You suggested that we have sex? Are you also controlling me to like you? What about the hunt for the Qilin? I always had questions about it being morally okay. Did you handle those qualms as well?" She stepped away from Apollo and clutched at her arms.

Apollo tried to talk, but could only stutter out a "no."

"It is true then. You just controlled me."

Reaching for her, Apollo was turned down again. Sadly, he let his hand drop. "I didn't make you love me. I can't do that. Sure, I suggested that we have sex and hunt the Qilin, but it was ultimately your choice. You had to want to do both of those things at least a little. I just tipped the scales in my favor."

Phoebe picked up the weapons bag and pulled out a blanket. Throwing it at Supay to wear, she walked away. "I don't want to see, hear, or speak to either of you again. Don't come after me," she called back to them. Reaching the street, she got on the first bus she saw and let it take her wherever it was going.

Chapter Two

Over the next few days, Phoebe went home and put all of her things in storage. She packed a bag and went to the airport. Not caring where she went, she bought the first ticket anywhere. Before long, she was sitting on a beach in Puerto Rico. Checking into the hotel under an assumed name, she immediately hit the bar.

Only a couple of months ago, she had found out that she was a daemon and that a new leader would bring peace. She thought that she was helping by finding the Qilin, but was betrayed by the man she was starting to love. Even worse, she was betrayed by her dog. This had to be a new low for humanity. Man's best friend turned out to be a shape shifter. Sighing, she sidled up onto the barstool. Next to her, a dark haired man was starting his first beer.

"Hey, did you just get here?" he asked Phoebe. She started and he motioned to her purse. "The tag from the airlines is still on your bag. Mind if I buy you a drink?"

Phoebe shrugged. She may as well have some fun. All she wanted right now was to get her mind off of the last few months. A few drinks and a one-night stand may be just what she needed. "Sure, can you get me a mojito?"

"Sure, that sounds great. What's your name?"

The man stretched out his hand to shake Phoebe's hand. "I am Peter. I just arrived in town to check on a factory in the area. What brings you here? You don't look like a business traveler, but you don't seem happy enough to be a tourist."

"It doesn't really matter. I just wanted to get away somewhere for a while." She finished her mojito and ordered another.

"Divorce?"

"No, I'd rather not talk about it." In reality, who would even believe her story? She'd probably end up in an insane asylum somewhere. "Can I buy you a drink?" Touching his shoulder slightly, she waited to see what he was thinking. Thoughts of her naked filled his mind. Smiling to herself, she ordered Peter a double.

"Whoa, whoa, why are we drinking so fast? Are you trying to get me drunk?" Peter joked.

She motioned to the drink. "Drink up, so I can take advantage of you later."

Peter started to laugh in response and then he realized she was serious. He paused for a moment, unaccustomed to women being this forward. Taking a gulp of his drink, he shrugged. "Sounds good to me. Is your hotel room around here?"

Phoebe nodded. "Just upstairs."

Together, they left the bar and took the elevator to her room. Peter tried to make small talk with Phoebe, but she was completely disinterested in talking. All she wanted was to relax, drink, and have sex until she could forget the betrayals of recent months. Entering the hotel room, she turned to Peter.

"Take off your clothes," she ordered. Without waiting for him to undress, she stripped her garments from her body and waited. Peter admired her taut body as he complied and took his clothes off. Throwing them in a pile on the floor, he moved forward. As his fingers touched her flesh, she jumped at the sudden human contact. He ran his fingers along her body and paused on her nipples. Peter groaned as he ran his fingers along her clit and realized how wet she was. Not wanting to wait, he threw her onto the bed and thrust his fingers into her. With his tongue, he played with her clit and caused her body to shudder as he touched her most sensitive spots. Wild excitement fueled her desire and she orgasmed within minutes, but it was not enough. She wanted more and could not let him leave without letting him orgasm as well. As she became more wet, Peter became crazed. Spreading her lips, he entered her without warning. The extended foreplay caused his cock to shake with anticipation and desire. A low moan escaped from his mouth as he drove into her. For a brief moment, Phoebe felt her soul separate from her body as her mind recognized the strangeness of having someone who was not Apollo above her. Throwing him off of her, she held her hand to her head as she tried to stop thinking about Apollo.

"Did I do something wrong?" Peter was concerned. It was odd that he should care so much about someone he just met and who was never going to talk to him again.

"No, I'm fine. Sorry, forget that I stopped. Here, let me go down on you." Kneeling next to the bed, she took his organ into her mouth and tasted herself on him. Peter let out a moan and Phoebe could feel his pulse quickening within his body. He twitched as she took him deeper into her mouth and she could feel his wiry tendons tightening as he came close to climax. Pushing her back, he tried to catch his breath.

"Wait one moment. I just…" he caught his breath, "I just need to pause for a moment so I don't come yet."

Lying next to him on the bed, Phoebe ran her hand tantalizingly up her body and started to gently finger herself. Next to her, Peter groaned.

"You can't do this to me. All you're doing is arousing me more." For a moment, he looked uncertain if he should try to abate his arousal or drive into her again. The moment of uncertainty passed quickly and he turned her over. Instead of playing with her clit, he moved further back. Surprised, Phoebe almost told him to stop. She had never had anal sex before, but the sudden sensation of pleasure doused any of her hesitation quickly. Pulling her hips toward him, he held on with an iron grip. As he entered her anal passage, Phoebe moaned in pleasure and in pain. Peter was already growing close to orgasm. The middle of his shaft was pulsating with energy and she could feel how much he wanted it. Within moments, she felt his face and chest against her back as his body fell onto her. She could feel the liquid welling up within her as he violently came. Finally finished, he fell back on the bed. His energy was spent and all that was left was a vivid satisfaction.

Standing up, Phoebe crossed the room and picked up his clothes. As she handed them to Peter, he looked at her in surprise. "You really weren't joking about just wanting sex, were you?"

She smiled pleasantly. "No, I wasn't. It truly has been a pleasure. Thank you."

Confused, Peter started to dress. "So, are you going to give me your number or e-mail address or anything?"

Shaking her head, she kissed him lightly on the cheek. Although he had used all of the sexual energy he possessed, Peter felt a longing to start another round. Seeing that she wanted him to leave, he left the room.

Chapter Three

Days and weeks passed in quick succession, but Phoebe remained at the hotel. For several nights, she had to carefully dodge Peter. He kept knocking on her door or having the front desk call up to her room. Before long, he finally gave up and went home when his business trip ended. After several more hook-ups, Phoebe was starting to feel like she may be able to return to normal. The memory of Apollo controlling her mind was starting to fade. Locking her hotel room, she wandered down to the lobby. She purchased a sandwich from a convenience store as she ambled out to the beach.

Lying down under the sunshine, Phoebe pulled off her beach coverup and allowed the rays of sunlight to tan her skin. Almost asleep, she listened to music on her iPod until an obstruction got in the way of the sunlight, casting a shadow over her. Opening her eyes, she saw Supay standing before her.

Annoyed, she sat up. "What are you doing here? I would have thought that you understood that I wanted to be left alone." She fingered the jade necklace the Qilin gave her. It was possibly the only positive thing that came out of knowing Apollo.

Supay sat cheerfully on the beach. "You can't keep me away too long. Besides, I know you too well. At heart, you couldn't stay angry at someone forever."

The reminder that he knew her well made her frown. Supay only knew her because he had spent years living as her dog. He had known that her mind-reading abilities would draw her into the search for the Qilin. As a shape shifter, Supay had figured that remaining a dog would be the easiest way to keep an eye on her.

Sighing, he touched her arm. "Here, read my thoughts. There wasn't any malice or contrivance in being your dog. I just wanted to make sure you stayed safe. I was also hoping that I could save the Qilin, but that didn't work out so well."

As she touched his arm, Phoebe could see into his mind. Memories of her playing fetch with him as a dog and cuddling at night entered her mind. Throughout the memories, she did not see anything close to malice. He may have chosen the wrong way to protect her, but it seemed like he truly meant it.

"Fine, so you didn't mean it to be malicious. I understand that. But don't you think it is a little weird for you to spend years living with me in secret? Or a major invasion of my privacy? How many times did I change in front of you without knowing that you weren't an actual dog."

Supay winked. "On the bright side, you have nothing to be embarrassed about in that department. You look amazing naked."

Phoebe snorted and rolled her eyes. "You aren't making your case look any better."

Supay pulled his hands back in mock exasperation. "Fine, fine, you're right. Let me make it up to you with a dinner?"

"You really think that will work?"

Smiling, Supay shook his head. "No, I didn't think it would work romantically. Unfortunately, I need to ask for your help with a daemon problem."

Sighing, Phoebe nodded. "I'll listen to what you have to say. Meet me at six, and you better take me someplace decent. Worst case scenario, I'll end up more annoyed at you and enjoy a good dinner."

Chapter Four

Hours later, Phoebe finished applying a layer of lipstick. Her lips stood out lusciously from the tanned skin on her face. Pausing, she fixed her red dress and pulled on a pair of stilettos. She may still have been angry at Supay, but she also wanted a chance to dress up. Over the last few weeks, she had missed having a close friend to talk to. Before she left the room, she put on her jade necklace as a kind of talisman to ward off any trouble.

Walking into the lobby, Phoebe caught sight of Supay immediately. It seemed like every female in the world couldn't stop staring at him. In a dark shirt and slacks, he looked like he had stepped out of a fashion magazine or spent his life as a high-powered CEO. Some of his chest hair curled enticingly out of his partially-buttoned shirt.

Phoebe walked over to Supay. "And I was worried that I would be overdressed. Are you sure that you don't have any romantic intentions?"

Supay laughed. "I only said that it wasn't going to be a romantic dinner—my intentions are still all my own. I take it from what you just said that you like the way I look?"

Rolling her eyes, Phoebe allowed him to open the door of a cab. Before long, they were at a restaurant. He had selected a delicious Italian eatery for their dinner. After ordering some wine, breadsticks, and the meal, Supay finally got down to business.

"Okay, so I still need your help. The Qilin thing didn't work—Apollo is no more a leader now than he was before. Unfortunately, the infighting among the daemon has actually changed. There have been arguments and small-scale battles that have resulted in death."

Phoebe took a bite of a bread stick. "How could I help? And why isn't Apollo doing anything?"

Supay shrugged. "Beats me. I never liked the guy. Anyone who is willing to kill an innocent person is not a good person in my book. I don't know if he is upset at losing you or realized that he may have killed the Qilin without a reason. Either way, he spends most of his time drinking and isn't helping."

Phoebe sat for a moment and thought about what Supay had just told her. She was still upset with Apollo, and she did not want to hear how troubled he was. "If you want help, I will help. By the way, what type of daemon are you? We never really talked before."

"My ancestors used to live in Peru. When the Spaniards came, many of our daemons ended up dying from smallpox and battles just like the humans in the area. I was named for the god of death."

"The god of death?" Phoebe stared at him.

"Yes, but it isn't what you think. The god of death, Supay, was viewed as a natural part of life. He was given offerings and gifts to ease the passage into the spirit world. On occasion he was feared, but not as much as you would think."

"That's... interesting."

Supay smiled. "Do you know which god you were named for?"

She shook her head. Since finding out she was a daemon, she had thought about looking it up. For some reason, she had just never gotten around to it.

"In Greek mythology, Phoebe was one of the original titans. At one point in time, she was known as the goddess of prophecy and oracular intellect. Considering your mind-reading abilities, you were aptly named. Your sister's name, Cassandra, was based off of a prophetess who was cursed with seeing the future and having no one believe her. If Apollo had thought more before listening to her prophecy about the Qilin, he would have realized how unlikely her prophecy was exact or even true."

Phoebe nodded. Her sister, Cassandra, was a twin that never survived birth. Rhea, her mother, had named her anyways and listened to her prophecy in a dream. "So you think that the prophecy that the death of the Qilin would show a great leader is not true?"

Supay shrugged. "Maybe it is. If it is true, it doesn't mean that the person who killed her will be the leader. It could be someone like you who was involved or even mean that the death set off a domino effect that shows the great leader. Or the prophecy could just be completely untrue."

Reaching into his pocket, Supay pulled out his wallet to pay the bill. As they left the restaurant, he called a cab. Phoebe turned to him. "You know, I can find my way home on my own. Dinner was great, thank you."

Supay laughed. "You can't get rid of me that easily. I spent years around you making sure you were safe. I am at least going to take you back to your hotel."

Together, they got into the cab. Both daemons were silent as the taxi sped through the traffic lights. Supay turned to Phoebe. "So are you going to stay here forever then? What do you plan on doing?"

Phoebe paused. "I'm not really sure. I just needed time away for a while. Soon, I may just return home and open up the fortune telling shop again. Returning to normal life could be a positive development for me."

Supay got out of the taxi and walked around the vehicle to open the door. Phoebe smiled at his gesture of chivalry. "Thanks." She looked back at the taxi. "Did you want to come up for a few minutes or do you need to leave right away?"

"I could come up." Arm in arm, they took the elevator up to her floor. On entering the room, Supay paused. For once, he was not sure what to do. His natural confidence died away as he waited to see if Phoebe wanted to talk or if she wanted him there for another reason. He was about to ask her when she turned toward him and gave him a kiss. Without having to think about it, Supay kissed her back. Years spent waiting for this moment fell away in an instant as he threw her against the wall. Pinning her arms behind her head, he ran his moist, warm lips along her neckline. Phoebe moaned in pleasure and reached to unbutton his shirt. Instead of letting her, he picked up one of the scarves from her suitcase.

"I can't let you have me that easily," he smiled charmingly. Tying her hands behind her back, Supay used another scarf to blindfold her eyes. "Let's make this last for as long as possible. Here, I have an idea. You stay here and I will be right back. Don't move or I will punish you."

Supay left the room and Phoebe waited patiently. The extra time spent waiting and anticipating had only made her more amorous. Supay removed her blindfold and she could see the muscles moving underneath his shirt. In his hand, he held a paint set.

"A paint set?" she asked.

"I want to paint your body and make you wait longer. I have all night to keep you waiting." Leaning forward, he pulled his pocket knife and cut down the center of her dress. The red fabric fell away and revealed the black lingerie she had chosen. Supay gave an appreciative moan as his finger traced the line where her bra covered her breast. Leaning forward, he pulled the breast out of the cup and held it admiringly in one hand. He placed his mouth sensually on her nipple and sucked. Without realizing it, he had pressed his body against her leg while he licked her nipple and she could feel his cock harden through his pants.

With obvious effort, Supay stepped back and stopped playing with her nipples. "Come, let's untie you temporarily so I can remove all of your clothes." Untying her hands, he let her step out of her dress completely. Instead of helping her, he just watched as her breasts bounced out of their cups. He had her lie down on the bed with her face on the sheets. Picking up the paintbrush, he started to paint her body with images from old tapestries. The brush gently titillated her skin and caused her hair to stand on end. Every few moments, he would lean in closer for a kiss. Instead of dimming her passion or causing her to grow tired, the movements of the brush only caused her to want him more. Turning over suddenly, she caught him between her legs and pulled him toward her. Trapped by her legs, his cock was against her. Supay tried to turn, but she had him in her grasp.

"What?" she asked innocently. "Don't tell me that you don't want me."

Groaning with pent-up desire, Supay gave in. In a fluid motion, he removed all of his clothes. His chest and arm muscles were well-defined from years of working out. Before she could truly admire him naked, he entered her in a sharp thrust. The instantaneous pleasure was unlike anything she had ever felt. Each thrust seemed to reach the core of her being and all she wanted was more. Moaning, she clasped him into her deeper and deeper.

Panting, Supay leaned back on his heels and pulled her on top of him. His arms lifted her between each thrust so that he was almost entirely outside of her body for a moment. Feeling his body quake inside of her, Phoebe realized that they were both close to orgasm. Supay started to reach for a condom, but she shook her head. "You don't need that. I can only get pregnant with another daemon from my tribe. Just stay in me the entire time."

She didn't have to tell him twice. Throwing her back on the bed again, he entered her violently. The bed shook against the wall as he thrust three times in succession. Bright lights exploded in her mind as she started to orgasm. The clenching of her muscles in orgasm brought Supay to orgasm with her. Hot fluid shot into her as she drifted away into ecstasy.

Moments passed and neither person could move. Glancing around, Phoebe realized that the paint from her back was all over the sheets. Clothes were strewn about the room in abandon. She laughed and curled up next to him. His flesh was still steamy and hot from lovemaking.

"So you want me to help you make peace with the daemons?" she asked faintly.

Supay kissed the top of her head. "Yes, if you are willing. The worst we can do is try. At best, we will actually be able to do it."

Looking up into his eyes, Phoebe gave him a long, passionate kiss. "I can do that. We will start tomorrow."

ROLLING OUT of bed, Phoebe looked on Supay's sleeping form. After spending several weeks with him in Puerto Rico, she decided to move back to Peru, where he lived for most of the year. Her life had taken a strange turn. Instead of working at her fortune telling shop, she was now essentially a kept woman. During the day, they worked together to stop the fighting that kept breaking out in the daemon world. The daemons were essentially a different type of human, and each daemon possessed a unique power. Phoebe could read minds, while Supay could transform into any animal. These unique abilities had given rise to the ancient mythologies of past years. In honor of their ancestors, Phoebe's daemon family had chosen to name all of their children after Greek gods and prophets.

Phoebe threw on a robe and turned on the shower. Over the last few months, she had learned that she was a daemon and that she still had a mother. Her mother, Rhea, had been raped and conceived twin girls. Her twin sister had never made it past birth, but Phoebe had been born. With her gift of mind-reading, she had been in constant pain as an infant because she could see her mother's memories of the rape. Traumatized by the rape and inability to touch her daughter, Rhea had placed Phoebe in foster care. Phoebe finally found out that she was a daemon and about the true story when Apollo came looking for help with killing the Qilin.

Stepping into the shower, Phoebe let the warm water drift along her body. The sensation was pleasant and woke her up. Today, she needed to go with Supay to meet a daemon called Juno. According to the reports, Juno was the daemon behind much of the infighting. With the death of the Qilin, a leader was supposed to appear that would bring peace. According to prophecy, it seemed like Apollo should have been that person. Since he was still brooding over beer about the loss of Phoebe and the killing of the Qilin, Supay had convinced Phoebe that they needed to take action together.

Phoebe heard the shower curtain open. Turning, she saw…

If you enjoyed this sample then look for **Forgotten - The Daemon Paranormal Romance Chronicles, Book 3**.

Here is a preview of **another story** you may enjoy:

Hunted - The Mind Talker Paranormal Romance Series, Book 2

WAKING UP was an experience for Jared. It had been years since he had felt an inkling of the comfort that is sleeping wrapped around someone he didn't have to worry about stabbing him in the back. It had been months since he last let his guard down enough to be intimate with anyone other than himself.

And yet this girl, someone who had never even been properly informed of what they were, had somehow blown clear past all of his defenses before he even realized they were down. It gave him an uneasy feeling the fact that he responded to her so quickly. He had thought himself incapable of feeling anything for another person other than hate and mistrust after all he had been through.

Jared's life wasn't rough in the beginning. He grew up in a normal household, with normal parents, a normal older sister and a normal dog. Overall his early life was completely and utterly normal. And then came puberty.

His freshman year of high school brought the normal bouts of acne and anger indicative of a boy on the journey of becoming a man. Being the nerd that he originally was, he had read every article and book on the subject that he could get his grubby little hands on, including some not so hidden Playboys that his dad kept stashed in a cooler in the garage. Everything that he had been experiencing was so tragically normal that it was almost a relief when he started hearing the voices. At first he thought himself crazy, maybe mad like the hatter from Alice and Wonderland; until the voices began to sound familiar. He could make out his sister's voice, shrill and lively even when muted. Then it was his parents. Soon he was hearing every thought contained in his high school and he realized what real crazy was.

It was a chilly day in November, the day before Thanksgiving break ironically, when one of his classmates, a boy who had been picked on and bullied for years and who Jared had been close acquaintances with moving in similar social circles, decided that he couldn't handle the pressure anymore. Jared had known that the boy, Kevin, was unstable just by listening to his rather disturbing thoughts day in and day out. He could hear the boy plotting something big, something that would stop his never-ending pain. Jared had known all this and yet he had done nothing. He was still getting a handle on control and though the boy's thoughts were filled with darkness, on the outside he appeared put together and in control. Jared feared that at best no one would believe him and at worst he'd put himself in harm's way if Kevin decided to take out his anger on him. So Jared stayed quiet, never even telling his sister, who was in the year above him, his concerns.

Jared had been sitting out on the lacrosse field where he normally took his lunch so he could avoid any awkwardness in the school cafeteria. His sister had often offered him a seat with her friends, but he usually turned her down in favor of his solo spot. It wasn't that he was anti-social, it's just that he knew one day he would grow into his looks and be, if not attractive, then at least average. However, he didn't want to sit for forty-five minutes and hear his sister's harpy friends with their high-pitched inner voices squawking and gushing over it. He thought that people who said women mature faster than men were horribly misinformed and probably home-schooled.

It was for this very reason that Jared heard rather than saw the commotion that happened without any warning. One minute he was biting into an apple, geometry book balanced on one knee, and the next he found himself sprawled on his side with his ears ringing as his lungs fought to pull in air. All around he could see bits of rock and drywall lying beside him and for one minute he wondered if he was dreaming. Slowly he started to make out the sounds of screams over his groans as he pushed his body up into a seated position. The scene that unfolded before him was straight out of a war movie.

If you enjoyed this sample then look for **Hunted - The Mind Talker Paranormal Romance Series, Book 2.**

Other Books by Darla Dunbar

- The Romeo Alpha BBW Paranormal Shifter Romance Series

- Romeo Alpha Blood Lines Romance

- The Alpha Feud BBW Paranormal Shifter Romance Series

- The Alpha Packed BBW Paranormal Shifter Romance Series

- The Mind Talker Paranormal Romance Series

- The Leather Satchel Paranormal Romance Series

Get the latest update on new releases from the author at:

https://darladunbar.com/newsletter/

About the Author - Darla Dunbar

Darla has been interested in paranormal romance since she was a teenager in high school. It was then that she discovered she could fulfill her fantasies through her writing.

Observing people and human behavior in the area of romance has always been one of her favorite pastimes. Combining that with an overactive imagination is a sure fire way of coming up with interesting themes.

Connect with Darla Dunbar

I really appreciate you reading my book! Here are my social media coordinates:

Friend me on Facebook: https://www.facebook.com/darladunbar/

Follow me on Twitter: https://twitter.com/DarlDunbar

Check me out on Goodreads: https://www.goodreads.com/author/show/8425857.Darl a_Dunbar

Subscribe to my newsletter: https://darladunbar.com/newsletter/

Visit my website: https://darladunbar.com/